In 1935 if you wanted to read a good book, you needed either a lot of money or a library card. Cheap paperbacks were available, but their poor production generally mirrored the quality between the covers. One weekend that year, Allen Lane, Managing Director of The Bodley Head, having spent the weekend visiting Agatha Christie, found himself on a platform at Exeter station trying to find something to read for his journey back to London. He was appalled by the quality of the material he had to choose from. Everything that Allen Lane achieved from that day until his death in 1970 was based on a passionate belief in the existence of 'a vast reading public for *intelligent* books at a low price'. The result of his momentous vision was the birth not only of Penguin, but of the 'paperback revolution'. Quality writing became available for the price of a packet of cigarettes, literature became a mass medium for the first time, a nation of book-borrowers became a nation of book-buyers – and the very concept of book publishing was changed for ever. Those founding principles – of quality and value, with an overarching belief in the fundamental importance of reading – have guided everything the company has done since 1935. Sir Allen Lane's pioneering spirit is still very much alive at Penguin in

th

MORE THAN A BUSINESS

'We decided it was time to end the almost customary half-hearted manner in which cheap editions were produced – as though the only people who could possibly want cheap editions must belong to a lower order of intelligence. We, however, believed in the existence in this country of a vast reading public for intelligent books at a low price, and staked everything on it'
Sir Allen Lane, 1902–1970

'The Penguin Books are splendid value for sixpence, so splendid that if other publishers had any sense they would combine against them and suppress them'
George Orwell

'More than a business ... a national cultural asset'
Guardian

'When you look at the whole Penguin achievement you know that it constitutes, in action, one of the more democratic successes of our recent social history'
Richard Hoggart

The Unabridged Pocketbook of Lightning

JONATHAN SAFRAN FOER

PENGUIN BOOKS

PENGUIN BOOKS

Published by the Penguin Group
Penguin Books Ltd, 80 Strand, London WC2R 0RL, England
Penguin Group (USA) Inc., 375 Hudson Street, New York, New York 10014, USA
Penguin Group (Canada), 10 Alcorn Avenue, Toronto, Ontario, Canada M4V 3B2
(a division of Pearson Penguin Canada Inc.)
Penguin Ireland, 25 St Stephen's Green, Dublin 2, Ireland
(a division of Penguin Books Ltd)
Penguin Group (Australia), 250 Camberwell Road, Camberwell, Victoria 3124,
Australia (a division of Pearson Australia Group Pty Ltd)
Penguin Books India Pvt Ltd, 11 Community Centre,
Panchsheel Park, New Delhi – 110 017, India
Penguin Group (NZ), cnr Airborne and Rosedale Roads, Albany,
Auckland 1310, New Zealand (a division of Pearson New Zealand Ltd)
Penguin Books (South Africa) (Pty) Ltd, 24 Sturdee Avenue,
Rosebank 2196, South Africa

Penguin Books Ltd, Registered Offices: 80 Strand, London WC2R 0RL, England

www.penguin.com

'A Primer for the Punctuation of Heart Disease' first published
in the *New Yorker* magazine 2002
Extremely Loud and Incredibly Close first published in the
USA by Houghton Mifflin Co. 2005
First published in Great Britain by Hamish Hamilton 2005
This extract published as a Pocket Penguin 2005
1

Set in 10.5/12.5pt Monotype Dante
Typeset by Palimpsest Book Production Limited
Polmont, Stirlingshire
Printed in England by Clays Ltd, St Ives plc

Contents

Author's Note

'The Unabridged Pocketbook of Lightning' was the title of a poem that a friend of mine wrote in college. It was in a collection of his, titled *Mirror Sadness*. That title came from a list of sadnesses in a novel I was then writing, which was still untitled. The novel went on to be published, with the title *Everything is Illuminated*. My friend, David, was the most talented writer I knew – *so* talented, in fact, that he began to find it impossible to write. 'The Unabridged Pocketbook of Lightning' was one of his last poems.

I always knew I wanted to write something with the title 'The Unabridged Pocketbook of Lightning'. And I knew that David would give me his blessing to do so. There's no greater feeling than inspiring someone. That might even be the point of art. And I noticed, too, that the less David wrote, the more he wanted me to write. As if there were some cosmic constant that needed to be maintained. Or as if writing weren't something that one person does, but an ongoing communal project, expressed, at different moments, from different people. Maybe literature is like lava, formed by thousands of years of heat of pressure, but erupting only in instants, and only from the volcano's mouth.

For the last five years, I kept 'The Unabridged Pocketbook of Lightning' in that mental drawer of things that have no present use, but will be indispensable one day. Occasionally I would take it out and try to write something to fit it. But it was like trying to change the dimensions of my hand to fit a glove I liked. Using it now, without any obvious connection to the content of this book, is more like filling a glove with peanuts. Peanuts need to be held in something. A glove can hold peanuts. But a glove and peanuts were not made for each other.

Or maybe they were.

About the enclosed peanuts . . . To follow are a story and three excerpts from my forthcoming novel, *Extremely Loud and Incredibly Close*. The story, 'A Primer for the Punctuation of Heart Disease', was published in the *New Yorker* in 2003. It's one of a small handful of stories I've written, and I think it's fairly representative of my concerns as a writer: the difficulties of expression, family and love.

The excerpt is comprised of three chapters, representing each of the three voices in the novel. Given that these chapters are, for all intents and purposes, the first three chapters of the book, nothing is needed by way of background.

Jonathan Safran Foer
1 January 2005

A Primer for the Punctuation of Heart Disease

□ The 'silence mark' signifies an absence of language, and there is at least one on every page of the story of my family life. Most often used in the conversations I have with my grandmother about her life in Europe during the war, and in conversations with my father about our family's history of heart disease – we have forty-one heart attacks between us, and counting – the silence mark is a staple of familial punctuation. Note the use of silence in the following brief exchange, when my father called me at college, the morning of his most recent angioplasty:

'Listen,' he said, and then surrendered to a long pause, as if the pause were what I was supposed to listen to. 'I'm sure everything's gonna be fine, but I just wanted to let you know –'

'I already know,' I said.

'□'

'□'

'□'

'□'

'OK,' he said.

'I'll talk to you tonight,' I said, and I could hear, in the receiver, my own heartbeat.

He said, 'Yup.'

■ The 'willed silence mark' signifies an intentional silence, the conversational equivalent of building a wall over which you can't climb, through which you can't see, against which you break the bones of your hands and wrists. I often inflict willed silences upon my mother when she asks about my relationships with girls. Perhaps this is because I never have *relationships* with girls – only *relations*. It depresses me to think that I've never had sex with anyone who really loved me. Sometimes I wonder if having sex with a girl who doesn't love me is like felling a tree, alone, in a forest: no one hears about it; it didn't happen.

?? The 'insistent question mark' denotes one family member's refusal to yield to a willed silence, as in this conversation with my mother:

'Are you dating at all?'

'□'

'But you're seeing people, I'm sure. Right?'

'□'

'I don't get it. Are you ashamed of the girl? Are you ashamed of me?'

'■'

'??'

¡ As it visually suggests, the 'unxclamation point' is the opposite of an exclamation point; it indicates a whisper.

The best example of this usage occurred when I was a boy. My grandmother was driving me to a piano lesson, and the Volvo's wipers only moved the rain around. She turned down the volume of the second side of the seventh tape of an audio version of *Shoah*, put her hand on my cheek, and said, 'I hope that you never love anyone as much as I love you¡'

Why was she whispering? We were the only ones who could hear.

★

¡¡ Theoretically, the ‘extraunxclamation points’ would be used to denote twice an unxclamation point, but in practice any whisper that quiet would not be heard. I take comfort in believing that at least some of the silences in my life were really extraunxclamations.

!! The ‘extraexclamation points’ are simply twice an exclamation point. I’ve never had a heated argument with any member of my family. We’ve never yelled at each other, or disagreed with any passion. In fact, I can’t even remember a difference of opinion. There are those who would say that this is unhealthy. But, since it is the case, there exists only one instance of extraexclamation points in our family history, and they were uttered by a stranger who was vying with my father for a parking space in front of the National Zoo.

‘Give it up, fucker!!’ he hollered at my father, in front of my mother, my brothers, and me.

‘Well, I’m sorry,’ my father said, pushing the bridge of his glasses up his nose, ‘but I think it’s rather obvious that we arrived at this space first. You see, we were approaching from –’

‘Give . . . it . . . up . . . fucker!!’

‘Well, it’s just that I think I’m in the right on this particu—’

‘GIVE IT UP, FUCKER!!’

‘Give it up, Dad¡’ I said, suffering a minor coronary event as my fingers clenched his seat’s headrest.

‘Je-sus!’ the man yelled, pounding his fist against the outside of his car door. ‘Giveitupfucker!!’

Ultimately, my father gave it up, and we found a spot several blocks away. Before we got out, he pushed in the cigarette lighter, and we waited, in silence, as it got hot. When it popped out, he pushed it back in. ‘It’s never, ever worth it,’ he said, turning back to us, his hand against his heart.

*

~ Placed at the end of a sentence, the 'pedal point' signifies a thought that dissolves into a suggestive silence. The pedal point is distinguished from the ellipsis and the dash in that the thought it follows is neither incomplete nor interrupted but an outstretched hand. My younger brother uses these a lot with me, probably because he, of all the members of my family, is the one most capable of telling me what he needs to tell me without having to say it. Or, rather, he's the one whose words I'm most convinced I don't need to hear. Very often he will say, 'Jonathan~' and I will say, 'I know.'

A few weeks ago, he was having problems with his heart. A visit to his university's health center to check out some chest pains became a trip to the emergency room became a week in the intensive-care unit. As it turns out, he's been having one long heart attack for the last six years. 'It's nowhere near as bad as it sounds,' the doctor told my parents, 'but it's definitely something we want to take care of.'

I called my brother that night and told him that he shouldn't worry. He said, 'I know. But that doesn't mean there's nothing to worry about~'

'I know~' I said.

'I know~' he said.

'I~'

'I~'

'□'

Does my little brother have relationships with girls? I don't know.

↓ Another commonly employed familial punctuation mark, the 'low point', is used either in place – or for accentuation at the end – of such phrases as 'This is terrible,' 'This is irremediable,' 'It couldn't possibly be worse.'

'It's good to have somebody, Jonathan. It's necessary.'

'□'

'It pains me to think of you alone.'

'■↓'

'??↓'

Interestingly, low points always come in pairs in my family. That is, the acknowledgment of whatever is terrible and irremediable becomes itself something terrible and irremediable – and often worse than the original referent. For example, my sadness makes my mother sadder than the cause of my sadness does. Of course, her sadness then makes me sad. Thus is created a 'low-point chain': ↓↓↓↓↓ . . . ∞.

❄ The 'snowflake' is used at the end of a unique familial phrase – that is, any sequence of words that has never, in the history of our family life, been assembled as such. For example, 'I didn't die in the Holocaust, but all of my siblings did, so where does that leave me?❄' Or, 'My heart is no good, and I'm afraid of dying, and I'm also afraid of saying I love you.❄'

☺ The 'corroboration mark' is more or less what it looks like. But it would be a mistake to think that it simply stands in place of 'I agree,' or even 'Yes.' Witness the subtle usage in this dialogue between my mother and my father:

'Could you add orange juice to the grocery list, but remember to get the kind with reduced acid. Also some cottage cheese. And that bacon-substitute stuff. And a few Yahrzeit candles.'

'☺'

'The car needs gas. I need tampons.'

'☺'

'Is Jonathan dating anyone? I'm not prying, but I'm very interested.'

''

My father has suffered twenty-two heart attacks – more than the rest of us combined. Once, in a moment of frankness after his nineteenth, he told me that his marriage to my mother had been successful because he had become a yes-man early on.

'We've only had one fight,' he said. 'It was in our first week of marriage. I realized that it's never, ever worth it.'

My father and I were pulling weeds one afternoon a few weeks ago. He was disobeying his cardiologist's order not to pull weeds. The problem, the doctor says, is not the physical exertion but the emotional stress that weeding inflicts on my father. He has dreams of weeds sprouting from his body, of having to pull them, at the roots, from his chest. He has also been told not to watch Orioles games and not to think about the current Administration.

As we weeded, my father made a joke about how my older brother, who, barring a fatal heart attack, was to get married in a few weeks, had already become a yes-man. Hearing this felt like having an elephant sit on my chest – my brother, whom I loved more than I loved myself, was surrendering.

'Your grandfather was a yes-man,' my father added, on his knees, his fingers pushing into the earth, 'and your children will be yes-men.'

I've been thinking about that conversation ever since, and I've come to understand – with a straining heart – that I, too, am becoming a yes-man, and that, like my father's and my brother's, my surrender has little to do with the people I say yes to, or with the existence of questions at all. It has to do with a fear of dying, with rehearsal and preparation.

*

✂ 🕸 The 'severed web' is a Barely Tolerable Substitute, whose meaning approximates 'I love you,' and which can be used in place of 'I love you.' Other Barely Tolerable Substitutes include, but are not limited to:

→|←, which approximates 'I love you.'
👂□, which approximates 'I love you.'
🔒, which approximates 'I love you.'
✕✈, which approximates 'I love you.'

I don't know how many Barely Tolerable Substitutes there are, but often it feels as if they were everywhere, as if everything that is spoken and done – every 'Yup,' 'OK,' and 'I already know,' every weed pulled from the lawn, every sexual act – were just Barely Tolerable.

⁘ Unlike the colon, which is used to mark a major division in a sentence, and to indicate that what follows is an elaboration, summation, implication, etc., of what precedes, the 'reversible colon' is used when what appears on either side elaborates, summates, implicates, etc., what's on the other side. In other words, the two halves of the sentence explain each other, as in the cases of 'Mother::Me', and 'Father::Death'. Here are some examples of reversible sentences:

My eyes water when I speak about my family::I don't like to speak about my family.

I've never felt loved by anyone outside of my family::my persistent depression.

1938 to 1945::□.

Sex::yes.

My grandmother's sadness::my mother's sadness::my sadness:: the sadness that will come after me.

To be Jewish::to be Jewish.
Heart disease::yes.

← Familial communication always has to do with failures to communicate. It is common that in the course of a conversation one of the participants will not hear something that the other has said. It is also quite common that one of the participants will not understand what the other has said. Somewhat less common is one participant's saying something whose words the other understands completely but whose meaning is not understood at all. This can happen with very simple sentences, like 'I hope that you never love anyone as much as I love you¡'

But, in our best, least depressing moments, we *try* to understand what we have failed to understand. A 'backup' is used: we start again at the beginning, we replay what was missed and make an effort to hear what was meant instead of what was said:

'It pains me to think of you alone.'
'← It pains me to think of me without any grandchildren to love.'

{} A related set of marks, the 'should-have brackets', signify words that were not spoken but should have been, as in this dialogue with my father:

'Are you hearing static?'
{'I'm crying into the phone.}'
'Jonathan?'
'□'
'Jonathan~'
'■'
'??'
'I::not myself~'

'{A child's sadness is a parent's sadness.}'

'{A parent's sadness is a child's sadness.}'

'←'

'I'm probably just tiredi'

'{I never told you this, because I thought it might hurt you, but in my dreams it was *you*. Not me. *You* were pulling the weeds from my chest.}'

'{I want to love and be loved.}'

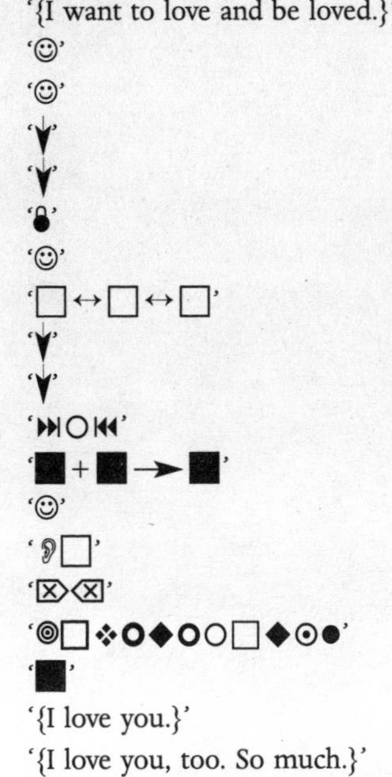

'{I love you.}'

'{I love you, too. So much.}'

Of course, my sense of the should-have is unlikely to be the same as my brothers', or my mother's, or my father's. Sometimes – when I'm in the car, or having sex, or talking to one of them on the phone – I imagine their should-have versions. I sew them together into a new life, leaving out everything that actually happened and was said. ◆

from *Extremely Loud and Incredibly Close*

What The?

What about a teakettle? What if the spout opened and closed when the steam came out, so it would become a mouth, and it could whistle pretty melodies, or do Shakespeare, or just crack up with me? I could invent a teakettle that reads in Dad's voice, so I could fall asleep, or maybe a set of kettles that sings the chorus of 'Yellow Submarine', which is a song by the Beatles, who I love, because entomology is one of my *raisons d'être*, which is a French expression that I know. Another good thing is that I could train my anus to talk when I farted. If I wanted to be extremely hilarious, I'd train it to say, 'Wasn't me!' every time I made an incredibly bad fart. And if I ever made an incredibly bad fart in the Hall of Mirrors, which is in Versailles, which is outside of Paris, which is in France, obviously, my anus would say, *'Ce n'était pas moi!'*

What about little microphones? What if everyone swallowed them, and they played the sounds of our hearts through little speakers, which could be in the pouches of our overalls? When you skateboarded down the street at night you could hear everyone's heartbeat, and they could hear yours, sort of like sonar. One weird thing is, I wonder if everyone's hearts would start to beat at the same time, like how women who live together have their menstrual periods at the same time, which I know about, but don't really want to know about. That would be so weird, except that the place in the hospital where babies are born would sound like a crystal chandelier in a houseboat, because the babies wouldn't have had time to match up their heartbeats yet. And at the finish line at the end of the New York City Marathon it would sound like war.

And also, there are so many times when you need to make a quick escape, but humans don't have their own wings, or not yet, anyway, so what about a birdseed shirt?

Anyway.

My first jujitsu class was three and a half months ago. Self-defense was something that I was extremely curious about, for obvious reasons, and Mom thought it would be good for me to have a physical activity besides tambourining, so my first jujitsu class was three and a half months ago. There were fourteen kids in the class, and we all had on neat white robes. We practiced bowing, and then we were all sitting down Native American style, and then Sensei Mark asked me to go over to him. 'Kick my privates,' he told me. That made me feel self-conscious. *'Excusez-moi?'* I told him. He spread his legs and told me, 'I want you to kick my privates as hard as you can.' He put his hands at his sides, and took a breath in, and closed his eyes, and that's how I knew that actually he meant business. 'Jose,' I told him, and inside I was thinking, *What the?* He told me, 'Go on, guy. Destroy my privates.' 'Destroy your privates?' With his eyes still closed he cracked up a lot and said, 'You couldn't destroy my privates if you tried. That's what's going on here. This is a demonstration of the well-trained body's ability to absorb a direct blow. Now destroy my privates.' I told him, 'I'm a pacifist,' and since most people my age don't know what that means, I turned around and told the others, 'I don't think it's right to destroy people's privates. Ever.' Sensei Mark said, 'Can I ask you something?' I turned back around and told him, '"Can I ask you something?" *is* asking me something.' He said, 'Do you have dreams of becoming a jujitsu master?' 'No,' I told him, even though I don't have dreams of running the family jewelry business anymore. He said, 'Do you want to know how a jujitsu student becomes a jujitsu master?' 'I want to know everything,' I told him, but that isn't true anymore either. He told me, 'A jujitsu student becomes a jujitsu master by destroying his master's privates.' I told him, 'That's fascinating.' My last jujitsu class was three and a half months ago.

I desperately wish I had my tambourine with me now, because even after everything I'm still wearing heavy boots, and sometimes it helps to play a good beat. My most impressive song that I can play on my tambourine is 'The Flight of the Bumblebee', by Nicolai Rimsky-Korsakov, which is also the ring tone I downloaded for the cell phone I got after Dad died. It's pretty amazing that I can play 'The Flight of the Bumblebee', because you have to hit incredibly fast in parts, and that's extremely hard for me, because I don't really have wrists yet. Ron offered to buy me a five-piece drum set. Money can't buy me love, obviously, but I asked if it would have Zildjian cymbals. He said, 'Whatever you want,' and then he took my yo-yo off my desk and started to walk the dog with it. I know he just wanted to be friendly, but it made me incredibly angry. 'Yo-yo *moi!*' I told him, grabbing it back. What I really wanted to tell him was 'You're not my dad, and you never will be.'

Isn't it so weird how the number of dead people is increasing even though the earth stays the same size, so that one day there isn't going to be room to bury anyone anymore? For my ninth birthday last year, Grandma gave me a subscription to *National Geographic*, which she calls 'the *National Geographic*'. She also gave me a white blazer, because I only wear white clothes, and it's too big to wear so it will last me a long time. She also gave me Grandpa's camera, which I loved for two reasons. I asked why he didn't take it with him when he left her. She said, 'Maybe he wanted you to have it.'

I said, 'But I was negative-thirty years old.' She said, 'Still.' Anyway, the fascinating thing was that I read in *National Geographic* that there are more people alive now than have died in all of human history. In other words, if everyone wanted to play Hamlet at once, they couldn't, because there aren't enough skulls!

So what about skyscrapers for dead people that were built down? They could be underneath the skyscrapers for living people that are built up. You could bury people one hundred floors down, and a whole dead world could be underneath the living one. Sometimes I think it would be weird if there were a skyscraper that moved up and down while its elevator stayed in place. So if you wanted to go to the ninety-fifth floor, you'd just press the 95 button and the ninety-fifth floor would come to you. Also, that could be extremely useful, because if you're on the ninety-fifth floor, and a plane hits below you, the building could take you to the ground, and everyone could be safe, even if you left your birdseed shirt at home that day.

I've only been in a limousine twice ever. The first time was terrible, even though the limousine was wonderful. I'm not allowed to watch TV at home, and I'm not allowed to watch TV in limousines either, but it was still neat that there was a TV there. I asked if we could go by school, so Toothpaste and The Minch could see me in a limousine. Mom said that school wasn't on the way, and we couldn't be late to the cemetery. 'Why not?' I asked, which I actually thought was a good question, because if you think about it, why not? Even though I'm not anymore, I used to be an atheist, which means I didn't believe in things that couldn't be observed. I believed that once you're dead, you're dead forever, and you don't feel anything, and you don't even dream. It's not that I believe in things that can't be observed now, because I don't. It's that I believe that things are extremely complicated. And anyway, it's not like we were *actually* burying him, anyway.

Even though I was trying hard for it not to, it was annoying me how Grandma kept touching me, so I climbed into the front seat and poked the driver's shoulder until he gave me some attention. 'What. Is. Your. Designation.' I asked in Stephen Hawking voice. 'Say what?' 'He wants to know your name,' Grandma said from the back seat. He handed me his card.

GERALD THOMPSON

Sunshine Limousine

serving the five boroughs

(212) 570-7249

I handed him my card and told him, 'Greetings. Gerald. I. Am. Oskar.' He asked me why I was talking like that. I told him, 'Oskar's CPU is a neural-net processor. A learning computer. The more contact he has with humans, the more he learns.' Gerald said, 'O' and then he said 'K.' I couldn't tell if he liked me or not, so I told him, 'Your sunglasses are one hundred dollars.' He said, 'One seventy-five.' 'Do you know a lot of curse words?' 'I know a couple.' 'I'm not allowed to use curse words.' 'Bummer.' 'What's "bummer"?' 'It's a bad thing.' 'Do you know "shit"?' 'That's a curse, isn't it?' 'Not if you say "shiitake."' 'Guess not.' 'Succotash my Balzac, dipshiitake.' Gerald shook his head and cracked up a little, but not in the bad way, which is at me. 'I can't even say "hair pie",' I told him, 'unless I'm talking about an actual pie made out of rabbits. Cool driving gloves.' 'Thanks.' And then I thought of something, so I said it. '*Actually*, if limousines were *extremely* long, they wouldn't *need* drivers. You could just get in the back seat, walk through the limousine, and then get out of the front seat, which would be where you wanted to go. So in this situation, the front seat would be at the cemetery.' 'And I would be watching the game right now.' I patted his shoulder and told him, 'When you look up "hilarious" in the dictionary, there's a picture of you.'

In the back seat, Mom was holding something in her purse. I could tell that she was squeezing it, because I could see her arm muscles. Grandma was knitting white mittens, so I knew they were for me, even though it wasn't cold out. I wanted to ask Mom what she was squeezing and why she had to keep it hidden. I remember thinking that even if I were suffering hypothermia, I would never, *ever* put on those mittens.

'Now that I'm thinking about it,' I told Gerald, 'they could make an *incredibly* long limousine that had its back seat at your mom's VJ and its front seat at your mausoleum, and it would be as long as your life.' Gerald said, 'Yeah, but if everyone lived like that, no one would ever meet anyone, right?' I said, 'So?'

Mom squeezed, and Grandma knitted, and I told Gerald, 'I kicked a French chicken in the stomach once,' because I wanted to make him crack up, because if I could make him crack up, my boots could be a little lighter. He didn't say anything, probably because he didn't hear me, so I said, 'I *said* I kicked a French chicken in the stomach once.' 'Huh?' 'It said, "*Oeuf*."' 'What is that?' 'It's a joke. Do you want to hear another, or have you already had *un oeuf*?' He looked at Grandma in the mirror and said, 'What's he saying?' She said, 'His grandfather loved animals more than he loved people.' I said, 'Get it? *Oeuf*?'

I crawled back, because it's dangerous to drive and talk at the same time, especially on the highway, which is what we were on. Grandma started touching me again, which was annoying, even though I didn't want it to be. Mom said, 'Honey,' and I said, '*Oui*,' and she said, 'Did you give a copy of our apartment key to the mailman?' I thought it was so weird that she would mention that then, because it didn't have to do with anything, but I think she was looking for something to talk about that wasn't the obvious thing. I said, 'The mailperson is a mail*woman*.' She nodded, but not exactly at me, and she asked if I'd given the mailwoman a key. I nodded yes, because I never used to lie to her before everything happened. I didn't have a reason to. 'Why did you do that?' she asked. So I told her, 'Stan –' And she said, 'Who?' And I said, 'Stan the doorman. Sometimes he runs around the corner for coffee, and I want to be sure all of my packages get to me, so I thought, if Alicia –' 'Who?' 'The mailwoman. If she had a key, she could leave things inside our door.' 'But you can't give a key to a stranger.' 'Fortunately Alicia isn't a stranger.' 'We have lots of valuable things in our apartment.' 'I know. We have really great things.' 'Sometimes people who seem good end up being not as good as you might have hoped, you know? What if she had stolen your things?' 'She wouldn't.' 'But what if?' 'But she wouldn't.' 'Well, did she give you a key to her apartment?' She was obviously mad at me, but I didn't know why. I hadn't done anything wrong. Or if I had, I didn't know what it was. And I definitely didn't mean to do it.

I moved over to Grandma's side of the limousine and told Mom, 'Why would I need a key to her apartment?' She could tell that I was zipping up the sleeping bag of myself, and I could tell that she didn't really love me. I knew the truth, which was that if she could have chosen, it would have been my funeral we were driving to. I looked up at the limousine's sunroof, and I imagined the world before there were ceilings, which made me wonder: Does a cave have no ceiling, or is a cave all ceiling? 'Maybe you could check with me next time, OK?' 'Don't be mad at me,' I said, and I reached over Grandma and opened and closed the door's lock a couple of times. 'I'm not mad at you,' she said. 'Not even a little?' 'No.' 'Do you still love me?' It didn't seem like the perfect time to mention that I had already made copies of the key for the deliverer from Pizza Hut, and the UPS person, and also the nice guys from Greenpeace, so they could leave me articles on manatees and other animals that are going extinct when Stan is getting coffee. 'I've never loved you more.'

'Mom?' 'Yes?' 'I have a question.' 'OK.' 'What are you squeezing in your purse?' She pulled out her hand and opened it, and it was empty. 'Just squeezing,' she said.

Even though it was an incredibly sad day, she looked so, so beautiful. I kept trying to figure out a way to tell her that, but all of the ways I thought of were weird and wrong. She was wearing the bracelet that I made for her, and that made me feel like one hundred dollars. I love making jewelry for her, because it makes her happy, and making her happy is another one of my *raisons d'être*.

It isn't anymore, but for a really long time it was my dream to take over the family jewelry business. Dad constantly used to tell me I was too smart for retail. That never made sense to me, because he was smarter than me, so if I was too smart for retail, then he *really* must have been too smart for retail. I told him that. 'First of all,' he told me, 'I'm not smarter than you, I'm more knowledgeable than you, and that's only because I'm older than you. Parents are always more knowledgeable than their children, and children are always smarter than their parents.' 'Unless the child is a mental retard,' I told him. He didn't have anything to say about that. 'You said "first of all", so what's second of all?' 'Second of all, if I'm so smart, then why am I in retail?' 'That's true,' I said. And then I thought of something: 'But wait a minute, it won't be the family jewelry business if no one in the family is running it.' He told me, 'Sure it will. It'll just be someone else's family.' I asked, 'Well, what about our family? Will we open a new business?' He said, 'We'll open something.' I thought about that my second time in a limousine, when the renter and I were on our way to dig up Dad's empty coffin.

A great game that Dad and I would sometimes play on Sundays was Reconnaissance Expedition. Sometimes the Reconnaissance Expeditions were extremely simple, like when he told me to bring back something from every decade in the twentieth century – I was clever and brought back a rock – and sometimes they were incredibly complicated and would go on for a couple of weeks. For the last one we ever did, which never finished, he gave me a map of Central Park. I said, 'And?' And he said, 'And what?' I said, 'What are the clues?' He said, 'Who said there had to be clues?' 'There are always clues.' 'That doesn't, in itself, suggest anything.' 'Not a single clue?' He said, 'Unless no clues is a clue.' 'Is no clues a clue?' He shrugged his shoulders, like he had no idea what I was talking about. I loved that.

I spent all day walking around the park, looking for something that might tell me something, but the problem was that I didn't know what I was looking for. I went up to people and asked if they knew anything that I should know, because sometimes Dad would design Reconnaissance Expeditions so I would have to talk to people. But everyone I went up to was just like, *What the?* I looked for clues around the reservoir. I read every poster on every lamppost and tree. I inspected the descriptions of the animals at the zoo. I even made kite-fliers reel in their kites so I could examine them, although I knew it was improbable. But that's how tricky Dad could be. There was nothing, which would have been unfortunate, unless nothing was a clue. Was nothing a clue?

That night we ordered General Tso's Gluten for dinner and I noticed that Dad was using a fork, even though he was perfect with chopsticks. 'Wait a minute!' I said, and stood up. I pointed at his fork. 'Is that fork a clue?' He shrugged his shoulders, which to me meant it was a major clue. I thought: *Fork, fork*. I ran to my laboratory and got my metal detector out of its box in the closet. Because I'm not allowed to be in the park alone at night, Grandma went with me. I started at the Eighty-sixth Street entrance and walked in extremely precise lines, like I was one of the Mexican guys who mow the lawn, so I wouldn't miss anything. I knew the insects were loud because it was summer, but I didn't hear them because my earphones covered my ears. It was just me and the metal underground.

Every time the beeps would get close together, I'd tell Grandma to shine the flashlight on the spot. Then I'd put on my white gloves, take the hand shovel from my kit, and dig extremely gently. When I saw something, I used a paintbrush to get rid of the dirt, just like a real archeologist. Even though I only searched a small area of the park that night, I dug up a quarter, and a handful of paper clips, and what I thought was the chain from a lamp that you pull to make the light go on, and a refrigerator magnet for sushi, which I know about, but wish I didn't. I put all of the evidence in a bag and marked on a map where I found it.

When I got home, I examined the evidence in my laboratory under my microscope, one piece at a time: a bent spoon, some screws, a pair of rusty scissors, a toy car, a pen, a key ring, broken glasses for someone with incredibly bad eyes . . .

I brought them to Dad, who was reading the *New York Times* at the kitchen table, marking the mistakes with his red pen. 'Here's what I've found,' I said, pushing my pussy off the table with the tray of evidence. Dad looked at it and nodded. I asked, 'So?' He shrugged his shoulders like he had no idea what I was talking about, and he went back to the paper. 'Can't you even tell me if I'm on the right track?' Buckminster purred, and Dad shrugged his shoulders again. 'But if you don't tell me anything, how can I ever be right?' He circled something in an article and said, 'Another way of looking at it would be, how could you ever be wrong?'

He got up to get a drink of water, and I examined what he'd circled on the page, because that's how tricky he could be. It was in an article about the girl who had disappeared, and how everyone thought the congressman who was humping her had killed her. A few months later they found her body in Rock Creek Park, which is in Washington, D.C., but by then everything was different, and no one cared anymore, except for her parents.

> statement, read to the hundreds of gathered press from a makeshift media center off the back of the family home, Levy's father adamantly restated his confidence that his daughter would be found. 'We will not stop looking until we are given a definitive reason to stop looking, namely, Chandra's return.' During the brief question and answer period that followed, a reporter from *El Pais* asked Mr Levy if by 'return' he meant 'safe return.' Overcome with emotion, Mr Levy was unable to speak, and his lawyer took the microphone.

> 'We continue to hope and pray for Chandra's safety, and will do everything within

It wasn't a mistake! It was a message to me!

I went back to the park every night for the next three nights. I dug up a hair clip, and a roll of pennies, and a thumbtack, and a coat hanger, and a 9V battery, and a Swiss Army knife, and a tiny picture frame, and a tag for a dog named Turbo, and a square of aluminum foil, and a ring, and a razor, and an extremely old pocket watch that was stopped at 5:37, although I didn't know if it was A.M. or P.M. But I still couldn't figure out what it all meant. The more I found, the less I understood.

I spread the map out on the dining room table, and I held down the corners with cans of V8. The dots from where I'd found things looked like the stars in the universe. I connected them, like an astrologer, and if you squinted your eyes like a Chinese person, it kind of looked like the word 'fragile'. Fragile. What was fragile? Was Central Park fragile? Was nature fragile? Were the things I found fragile? A thumbtack isn't fragile. Is a bent spoon fragile? I erased, and connected the dots in a different way, to make 'door'. Fragile? Door? Then I thought of *porte*, which is French for door, obviously. I erased and connected the dots to make '*porte*'. I had the revelation that I could connect the dots to make 'cyborg', and 'platypus', and 'boobs', and even 'Oskar', if you were extremely Chinese. I could connect them to make almost anything I wanted, which meant I wasn't getting closer to anything. And now I'll never know what I was supposed to find. And that's another reason I can't sleep.

Anyway.

I'm not allowed to watch TV, although I am allowed to

rent documentaries that are approved for me, and I can read anything I want. My favorite book is *A Brief History of Time*, even though I haven't actually finished it, because the math is incredibly hard and Mom isn't good at helping me. One of my favorite parts is the beginning of the first chapter, where Stephen Hawking tells about a famous scientist who was giving a lecture about how the earth orbits the sun, and the sun orbits the solar system, and whatever. Then a woman in the back of the room raised her hand and said, 'What you have told us is rubbish. The world is really a flat plate supported on the back of a giant tortoise.' So the scientist asked her what the tortoise was standing on. And she said, 'But it's turtles all the way down!'

I love that story, because it shows how ignorant people can be. And also because I love tortoises.

A few weeks after the worst day, I started writing lots of letters. I don't know why, but it was one of the only things that made my boots lighter. One weird thing is that instead of using normal stamps, I used stamps from my collection, including valuable ones, which sometimes made me wonder if what I was really doing was trying to get rid of things. The first letter I wrote was to Stephen Hawking. I used a stamp of Alexander Graham Bell.

Dear Stephen Hawking,

Can I please be your protégé?

Thanks,

Oskar Schell

I thought he wasn't going to respond, because he was such an amazing person and I was so normal. But then one day I came home from school and Stan handed me an envelope and said, 'You've got mail!' in the AOL voice I taught him. I ran up the 105 stairs to our apartment, and ran to my laboratory, and went into my closet, and turned on my flashlight, and opened it. The letter inside was typed, obviously, because Stephen Hawking can't use his hands, because he has amyotrophic lateral sclerosis, which I know about, unfortunately.

> *Thank you for your letter. Because of the large volume of mail I receive, I am unable to write personal responses. Nevertheless, know that I read and save every letter, with the hope of one day being able to give each the proper response it deserves. Until that day,*
>
> *Most sincerely,*
> *Stephen Hawking*

I called Mom's cell. 'Oskar?' 'You picked up before it rang.' 'Is everything OK?' 'I'm gonna need a laminator.' 'A laminator?' 'There's something incredibly wonderful that I want to preserve.'

Dad always used to tuck me in, and he'd tell the greatest stories, and we'd read the *New York Times* together, and sometimes he'd whistle 'I Am the Walrus', because that was his favorite song, even though he couldn't explain what it meant, which frustrated me. One thing that was so great was how he could find a mistake in every single article we looked at. Sometimes they were grammar mistakes, sometimes they were mistakes with geography or facts, and sometimes the article just didn't tell the whole story. I loved having a dad who was smarter than the *New York Times*, and I loved how my cheek could feel the hairs on his chest through his T-shirt, and how he always smelled like shaving, even at the end of the day. Being with him made my brain quiet. I didn't have to invent a thing.

When Dad was tucking me in that night, the night before the worst day, I asked if the world was a flat plate supported on the back of a giant tortoise. 'Excuse me?' 'It's just that why does the earth stay in place instead of falling through the universe?' 'Is this Oskar I'm tucking in? Has an alien stolen his brain for experimentation?' I said, 'We don't believe in aliens.' He said, 'The earth *does* fall through the universe. You know that, buddy. It's constantly falling toward the sun. That's what it means to orbit.' So I said, 'Obviously, but why is there gravity?' He said, 'What do you mean why is there gravity?' 'What's the reason?' 'Who said there had to be a reason?' 'No one did, exactly.' 'My question was rhetorical.' 'What's that mean?' 'It means I wasn't asking it for an answer, but to make a point.' 'What point?' 'That there doesn't have to be a reason.' 'But if there isn't a reason, then why does the universe exist at all?' 'Because of sympathetic conditions.' 'So then why am I your son?' 'Because Mom and I made love, and one of my sperm fertilized one of her eggs.' 'Excuse me while I regurgitate.' 'Don't act your age.' 'Well, what I don't get is why do we exist? I don't mean how, but why.' I watched the fireflies of his thoughts orbit his head. He said, 'We exist because we exist.' '*What the?*' 'We could imagine all sorts of universes unlike this one, but this is the one that happened.'

I understood what he meant, and I didn't disagree with him, but I didn't agree with him either. Just because you're an atheist, that doesn't mean you wouldn't love for things to have reasons for why they are.

I turned on my shortwave radio, and with Dad's help I was able to pick up someone speaking Greek, which was nice. We couldn't understand what he was saying, but we lay there, looking at the glow-in-the-dark constellations on my ceiling, and listened for a while. 'Your grandfather spoke Greek,' he said. 'You mean he *speaks* Greek,' I said. 'That's right. He just doesn't speak it here.' 'Maybe that's him we're listening to.' The front page was spread over us like a blanket. There was a picture of a tennis player on his back, who I guess was the winner, but I couldn't really tell if he was happy or sad.

'Dad?' 'Yeah?' 'Could you tell me a story?' 'Sure.' 'A good one?' 'As opposed to all the boring ones I tell.' 'Right.' I tucked my body incredibly close into his, so my nose pushed into his armpit. 'And you won't interrupt me?' 'I'll try not to.' 'Because it makes it hard to tell a story.' 'And it's annoying.' 'And it's annoying.'

The moment before he started was my favorite moment.

'Once upon a time, New York City had a sixth borough.' 'What's a borough?' 'That's what I call an interruption.' 'I know, but the story won't make any sense to me if I don't know what a borough is.' 'It's like a neighborhood. Or a collection of neighborhoods.' 'So if there was once a sixth borough, then what are the five boroughs?' 'Manhattan, obviously, Brooklyn, Queen, Staten Island, and the Bronx.' 'Have I ever been to any of the other boroughs?' 'Here we go.' 'I just want to know.' 'We went to the Bronx Zoo once, a few years ago. Remember that?' 'No.' 'And we've been to Brooklyn to see the roses at the Botanic Garden.' 'Have I been to Queens?' 'I don't think so.' 'Have I been to Staten Island?' 'No.' 'Was there *really* a sixth borough?' 'I've been trying to tell you.' 'No more interruptions. I promise.'

When the story finished, we turned the radio back on and found someone speaking French. That was especially nice, because it reminded me of the vacation we just came back from, which I wish never ended. After a while, Dad asked me if I was awake. I told him no, because I knew that he didn't like to leave until I had fallen asleep, and I didn't want him to be tired for work in the morning. He kissed my forehead and said good night, and then he was at the door.

'Dad?' 'Yeah, buddy?' 'Nothing.'

The next time I heard his voice was when I came home from school the next day. We were let out early, because of what happened. I wasn't even a little bit panicky, because both Mom and Dad worked in midtown, and Grandma didn't work, obviously, so everyone I loved was safe.

I know that it was 10:18 when I got home, because I look at my watch a lot. The apartment was so empty and so quiet. As I walked to the kitchen, I invented a lever that could be on the front door, which would trigger a huge spoked wheel in the living room to turn against metal teeth that would hang down from the ceiling, so that it would play beautiful music, like maybe 'Fixing a Hole' or 'I Want to Tell You', and the apartment would be one huge music box.

After I petted Buckminster for a few seconds, to show him I loved him, I checked the phone messages. I didn't have a cell phone yet, and when we were leaving school, Toothpaste told me he'd call to let me know whether I was going to watch him attempt skateboarding tricks in the park, or if we were going to go look at *Playboy* magazines in the drugstore with the aisles where no one can see what you're looking at, which I didn't feel like doing, but still.

Message one. Tuesday, 8:52 A.M. *Is anybody there? Hello? It's Dad. If you're there, pick up. I just tried the office, but no one was picking up. Listen, something's happened. I'm OK. They're telling us to stay where we are and wait for the firemen. I'm sure it's fine. I'll give you another call when I have a better idea of what's going on. Just wanted to let you know that I'm OK, and not to worry. I'll call again soon.*

There were four more messages from him: one at 9:12, one at 9:31, one at 9:46, and one at 10:04. I listened to them, and listened to them again, and then before I had time to figure out what to do, or even what to think or feel, the phone started ringing.

It was 10:22:27.

I looked at the caller ID and saw that it was him.

Why I'm Not Where You Are
5/21/63

To my unborn child: I haven't always been silent, I used to talk and talk and talk and talk, I couldn't keep my mouth shut, the silence overtook me like a cancer, it was one of my first meals in America, I tried to tell the waiter, 'The way you just handed me that knife, that reminds me of –' but I couldn't finish the sentence, her name wouldn't come, I tried again, it wouldn't come, she was locked inside me, how strange, I thought, how frustrating, how pathetic, how sad, I took a pen from my pocket and wrote 'Anna' on my napkin, it happened again two days later, and then again the following day, she was the only thing I wanted to talk about, it kept happening, when I didn't have a pen, I'd write 'Anna' in the air – backward and right to left – so that the person I was speaking with could see, and when I was on the phone I'd dial the numbers – 2, 6, 6, 2 – so that the person could hear what I couldn't, myself, say. 'And' was the next word I lost, probably because it was so close to her name, what a simple word to say, what a profound word to lose, I had to say 'ampersand', which sounded ridiculous, but there it is, 'I'd like a coffee ampersand something sweet,' nobody would choose to be like that. 'Want' was a word I lost early on, which is not to say that I stopped wanting things – I wanted things more – I just stopped being able to express the want, so instead I said 'desire', 'I desire two rolls,' I would tell the baker, but that wasn't quite right, the meaning of my thoughts started to float away from me, like leaves that fall from a tree into a river, I was the tree, the world was the river. I lost 'come' one afternoon with the dogs in the park, I lost 'fine' as the barber turned me toward the mirror, I lost 'shame' – the verb and the noun in the same moment; it was a shame. I lost 'carry', I lost the things I carried – 'daybook', 'pencil', 'pocket change', 'wallet' – I even lost 'loss'. After a time, I had only a handful of words left, if someone did something nice for me, I would tell him, 'The thing that comes before "you're welcome",' if I was hungry, I'd point at my stomach and say, 'I am the opposite of full,' I'd lost 'yes', but I still had 'no', so if someone asked me, 'Are you Thomas?' I would answer, 'Not no,' but then I lost 'no', I went to a tattoo parlor and had YES written onto the palm of my left hand, and NO onto my right palm, what can I say, it hasn't made life wonderful, it's made life possible, when I rub my hands against each other in the middle of winter I am warming myself with the friction of YES and NO, when I clap my hands I am showing my appreciation through the uniting and parting of YES and NO, I signify 'book' by peeling open my clapped hands, every book, for me, is the balance of YES and NO, even this one, my last one, especially this one. Does it break my heart, of course, every moment of every day, into more pieces than my heart was made of, I never thought of myself as quiet, much less silent, I never thought about things at all, everything changed, the distance that wedged itself between me and my happiness wasn't the world, it wasn't the bombs and burning buildings, it was me, my thinking, the cancer of never letting go, is ignorance bliss, I don't know, but it's so painful to think, and tell me, what did thinking ever do for me, to what great place did thinking ever bring me? I think and think and think, I've thought myself out of happiness one million times, but never once into it. 'I' was the last word I was able to speak aloud, which is a terrible thing, but there it is, I would walk around the neighborhood saying, 'I I I I.' 'You want a cup of coffee,

Thomas?' 'I.' 'And maybe something sweet?' 'I.' 'How about this weather?' 'I.' 'You look upset. Is anything wrong?' I wanted to say, 'Of course,' I wanted to ask, 'Is anything right?' I wanted to pull the thread, unravel the scarf of my silence and start again from the beginning, but instead I said, 'I.' I know I'm not alone in this disease, you hear the old people in the street and some of them are moaning, 'Ay yay yay,' but some of them are clinging to their last word, 'I,' they're saying, because they're desperate, it's not a complaint it's a prayer, and then I lost 'I' and my silence was complete. I started carrying blank books like this one around, which I would fill with all the things I couldn't say, that's how it started, if I wanted two rolls of bread from the baker, I would write 'I want two rolls' on the next blank page and show it to him, and if I needed help from someone, I'd write 'Help,' and if something made me want to laugh, I'd write 'Ha ha ha!' and instead of singing in the shower I would write out the lyrics of my favorite songs, the ink would turn the water blue or red or green, and the music would run down my legs, at the end of each day I would take the book to bed with me and read through the pages of my life:

*

I want two rolls

★

And I wouldn't say no to something sweet

★

I'm sorry, this is the smallest I've got

★

Start spreading the news . . .

★

The regular, please

*

Thank you, but I'm about to burst

*

I'm not sure, but it's late

*

Help

*

Ha ha ha!

It wasn't unusual for me to run out of blank pages before the end of the day, so should I have to say something to someone on the street or in the bakery or at the bus stop, the best I could do was flip back through the daybook and find the most fitting page to recycle, if someone asked me, 'How are you feeling?' it might be that my best response was to point at, 'The regular, please,' or perhaps, 'And I wouldn't say no to something sweet,' when my only friend, Mr Richter, suggested, 'What if you tried to make a sculpture again? What's the worst thing that could happen?' I shuffled halfway into the filled book: 'I'm not sure, but it's late.' I went through hundreds of books, thousands of them, they were all over the apartment, I used them as doorstops and paperweights, I stacked them if I needed to reach something, I slid them under the legs of wobbly tables, I used them as trivets and coasters, to line the birdcages and to swat insects from whom I begged forgiveness, I never thought of my books as being special, only necessary, I might rip out a page – 'I'm sorry, this is the smallest I've got' – to wipe up some mess, or empty a whole day to pack up the emergency light bulbs, I remember spending an afternoon with Mr Richter in the Central Park Zoo, I went weighted down with food for the animals, only someone who'd never been an animal would put up a sign saying not to feed them, Mr Richter told a joke, I tossed hamburger to the lions, he rattled the cages with his laughter, the animals went to the corners, we laughed and laughed, together and separately, out loud and silently, we were determined to ignore whatever needed to be ignored, to build a new world from nothing if nothing in our world could be salvaged, it was one of the best days of my life, a day during which I lived my life and didn't think about my life at all. Later that year, when snow started to hide the front steps, when morning became evening as I sat on the sofa, buried under everything I'd lost, I made a fire and used my laughter for kindling: 'Ha ha ha!' 'Ha ha ha!' 'Ha ha ha!' 'Ha ha ha!' I was already out of words when I met your mother, that may have been what made our marriage possible, she never had to know me. We met at the Columbian Bakery on Broadway, we'd both come to New York lonely, broken and confused, I was sitting in the corner stirring cream into coffee, around and around like a little solar system, the place was half empty but she slid right up next to me, 'You've lost everything,' she said, as if we were sharing a secret, 'I can see.' If I'd been someone else in a different world I'd've done something different, but I was myself, and the world was the world, so I was silent, 'It's OK,' she whispered, her mouth too close to my ear, 'Me too. You can probably see it from across a room. It's not like being Italian. We stick out like sore thumbs. Look at how they look. Maybe they don't know that we've lost everything, but they know something's off.' She was the tree and also the river flowing away from the tree, 'There are worse things,' she said, 'worse than being like us. Look, at least we're alive,' I could see that she wanted those last words back, but the current was too strong, 'And the weather is one hundred dollars, also, don't let me forget to mention,' I stirred my coffee. 'But I hear it's supposed to get crummy tonight. Or that's what the man on the radio said, anyway,' I shrugged, I didn't know what 'crummy' meant, 'I was gonna go buy some tuna fish at the A&P. I clipped some coupons from the Post this morning. They're five cans for the price of three. What a deal! I don't even like tuna fish. It gives me stomachaches, to be frank. But you can't beat that price,' she was trying to make me laugh, but I shrugged my shoulders and stirred my coffee, 'I don't know anymore,' she said. 'The weather is one hundred dollars, and the man on the radio

says it's gonna get crummy tonight, so maybe I should go to the park instead, even if I burn easily. And anyway, it's not like I'm gonna eat the tuna fish tonight, right? Or ever, if I'm being frank. It gives me stomachaches, to be perfectly frank. So there's no rush in that department. But the weather, now that won't stick around. Or at least it never has. And I should tell you also that my doctor says getting out is good for me. My eyes are crummy, and he says I don't get out nearly enough, and that if I got out a little more, if I were a little less afraid . . .' She was extending a hand that I didn't know how to take, so I broke its fingers with my silence, she said, 'You don't want to talk to me, do you?' I took my daybook out of my knapsack and found the next blank page, the second to last. 'I don't speak,' I wrote. 'I'm sorry.' She looked at the piece of paper, then at me, then back at the piece of paper, she covered her eyes with her hands and cried, tears seeped between her fingers and collected in the little webs, she cried and cried and cried, there weren't any napkins nearby, so I ripped the page from the book – 'I don't speak. I'm sorry.' – and used it to dry her cheeks, my explanation and apology ran down her face like mascara, she took my pen from me and wrote on the next blank page of my daybook, the final one:

⋆

Please marry me

⋆

I flipped back and pointed at, 'Ha ha ha!' She flipped forward and pointed at, 'Please marry me.' I flipped back and pointed at, 'I'm sorry, this is the smallest I've got.' She flipped forward and pointed at, 'Please marry me.' I flipped back and pointed at, 'I'm not sure, but it's late.' She flipped forward and pointed at, 'Please marry me,' and this time put her finger on 'Please,' as if to hold down the page and end the conversation, or as if she were trying to push through the word and into what she really wanted to say. I thought about life, about my life, the embarrassments, the little coincidences, the shadows of alarm clocks on bedside tables. I thought about my small victories and everything I'd seen destroyed, I'd swum through mink coats on my parents' bed while they hosted downstairs, I'd lost the only person I could have spent my only life with, I'd left behind a thousand tons of marble, I could have released sculptures, I could have released myself from the marble of myself. I'd experienced joy, but not nearly enough, could there be enough? The end of suffering does not justify the suffering, and so there is no end to suffering, what a mess I am, I thought, what a fool, how foolish and narrow, how worthless, how pinched and pathetic, how helpless. None of my pets know their own names, what kind of person am I? I lifted her finger like a record needle and flipped back, one page at a time:

⋆

Help

⋆

My Feelings

12 September 2003
Dear Oskar,
I am writing this to you from the airport.
I have so much to say to you. I want to begin at the beginning, because that is what you deserve. I want to tell you everything, without leaving out a single detail. But where is the beginning? And what is everything?
I am an old woman now, but once I was a girl. It's true. I was a girl like you are a boy. One of my chores was to bring in the mail. One day there was a note addressed to our house. There was no name on it. It was mine as much as anyone's, I thought. I opened it. Many words had been removed from the text by a censor.
14 January 1921
To Whom Shall Receive This Letter:
My name is XXXXXXX XXXXXXXXX, and I am a XXXXXXXX in Turkish Labor Camp XXXXX, Block XX. I know that I am lucky XX X XXXXXXX to be alive at all. I have chosen to write to you without knowing who you are. My parents XXXXXXX XXX. My brothers and sisters XXXXX XXXX, the main XXXXXX XX XXXXXXXX! I have written XXX XX XXXXX XXXXXXX every day since I have been here. I trade bread for postage, but have not yet received a response. Sometimes it comforts me to think that they do not mail the letters we write.
XXX XX XXXXXX, or at least XXX XXXXXXXXX?
XX XXXXX X XX throughout XXXXX XX.

XXX XXX XX XXXXX, and XXXXX XX XXXXX XX XXX, without once XXX XX XXXXXX, XXX XXXXXXXX XXX XXXXX nightmare?
XXX XXX, XX XXXXX XX XXXXX XX! XXXXX XX XXX XX XXX XX XXXXXX to write a few words to me I would appreciate it more than you ever could know. Several of the XXXXXX XXXX received mail so I know that XX XX XXXXXXXX. Please include a picture of yourself as well as your name. Include everything.
With great hopes,
Sincerely I am,
XXXXXXXX XXXXXXXXX
I took the letter straight to my room. I put it under my mattress. I never told my father or mother about it. For weeks I was awake all night wondering. Why was this man sent to a Turkish labor camp? Why had the letter come fifteen years after it had been written? Where had it been for those fifteen years? Why hadn't anyone written back to him? The others got mail, he said. Why had he sent a letter to our house? How did he know the name of my street? How did he know of Dresden? Where did he learn German? What became of him?
I tried to learn as much about the man as I could from the letter. The words were very simple. Bread means only bread. Mail is mail. Great hopes are great hopes are great hopes. I was left with the handwriting.
So I asked my father, your great-grandfather, whom I considered the best, most kindhearted man I knew, to write a letter to me. I told him it didn't matter what he wrote about. Just write, I said. Write anything.
Darling,
You asked me to write you a letter, so I am writing you a letter. I do not know why I am writing this letter, or what

this letter is supposed to be about, but I am writing it nonetheless, because I love you very much and trust that you have some good purpose for having me write this letter. I hope that one day you will have the experience of doing something you do not understand for someone you love.
Your father
That letter is the only thing of my father's that I have left. Not even a picture.
Next I went to the penitentiary. My uncle was a guard there. I was able to get the handwriting sample of a murderer. My uncle asked him to write an appeal for early release. It was a terrible trick that we played on this man.
To the Prison Board:
My name is Kurt Schluter. I am Inmate 24922. I was put here in jail a few years ago. I don't know how long it's been. We don't have calendars. I keep lines on the wall with chalk. But when it rains, the rain comes through my window when I am sleeping. And when I wake up the lines are gone. So I don't know how long it's been.
I murdered my brother. I beat his head in with a shovel. Then after I used that shovel to bury him in the yard. The soil was red. Weeds came from the grass where his body was. Sometimes at night I would get on my knees and pull them out, so no one would know.
I did a terrible thing. I believe in the afterlife. I know that you can't take anything back. I wish that my days could be washed away like the chalk lines of my days.
I have tried to become a good person. I help the other inmates with their chores. I am patient now.
It might not matter to you, but my brother was having an affair with my wife. I didn't kill my wife. I want to go back to her, because I forgive her.
If you release me I will be a good person, quiet, out of the way.

Please consider my appeal.
Kurt Schluter, Inmate 24922
My uncle later told me that the inmate had been in prison for more than forty years. He had gone in as a young man. When he wrote the letter to me he was old and broken. His wife had remarried. She had children and grandchildren. Although he never said it, I could tell that my uncle had befriended the inmate. He had also lost a wife, and was also in a prison. He never said it, but I heard in his voice that he cared for the inmate. They guarded each other. And when I asked my uncle, several years later, what became of the inmate, my uncle told me that he was still there. He continued to write letters to the board. He continued to blame himself and forgive his wife, not knowing that there was no one on the other end. My uncle took each letter and promised the inmate that they would be delivered. But instead he kept them all. They filled all of the drawers in his dresser. I remember thinking it's enough to drive someone to kill himself. I was right. My uncle, your great-great-uncle, killed himself. Of course it's possible that the inmate had nothing to do with it.
With those three samples I could make comparisons. I could at least see that the forced laborer's handwriting was more like my father's than the murderer's. But I knew that I would need more letters. As many as I could get.
So I went to my piano teacher. I always wanted to kiss him, but was afraid he would laugh at me. I asked him to write a letter.
And then I asked my mother's sister. She loved dance but hated dancing.
I asked my schoolmate Mary to write a letter to me. She was funny and full of life. She liked to run around her empty house without any clothes on, even once she was too old for

that. Nothing embarrassed her. I admired that so much, because everything embarrassed me, and that hurt me. She loved to jump on her bed. She jumped on her bed for so many years that one afternoon, while I watched her jump, the seams burst. Feathers filled the small room. Our laughter kept the feathers in the air. I thought about birds. Could they fly if there wasn't someone, somewhere, laughing? I went to my grandmother, your great-great-grandmother, and asked her to write a letter. She was my mother's mother. Your father's mother's mother's mother. I hardly knew her. I didn't have any interest in knowing her. I have no need for the past, I thought, like a child. I did not consider that the past might have a need for me.
What kind of letter? my grandmother asked.
I told her to write whatever she wanted to write.
You want a letter from me? she asked.
I told her yes.
Oh, God bless you, she said.
The letter she gave me was sixty-seven pages long. It was the story of her life. She made my request into her own. Listen to me.
I learned so much. She sang in her youth. She had been to America as a girl. I never knew that. She had fallen in love so many times that she began to suspect she was not falling in love at all, but doing something much more ordinary. I learned that she never learned to swim, and for that reason she always loved rivers and lakes. She asked her father, my great-grandfather, your great-great-great-grandfather, to buy her a dove. Instead he bought her a silk scarf. So she thought of the scarf as a dove. She even convinced herself that it contained flight, but did not fly, because it did not want to show anyone what it really was. That was how much she loved her father.

The letter was destroyed, but its final paragraph is inside of me.

She wrote, I wish I could be a girl again, with the chance to live my life again. I have suffered so much more than I needed to. And the joys I have felt have not always been joyous. I could have lived differently. When I was your age, my grandfather bought me a ruby bracelet. It was too big for me and would slide up and down my arm. It was almost a necklace. He later told me that he had asked the jeweler to make it that way. Its size was supposed to be a symbol of his love. More rubies, more love. But I could not wear it comfortably. I could not wear it at all. So here is the point of everything I have been trying to say. If I were to give a bracelet to you, now, I would measure your wrist twice.

With love,

Your grandmother

I had a letter from everyone I knew. I laid them out on my bedroom floor, and organized them by what they shared. One hundred letters. I was always moving them around, trying to make connections. I wanted to understand. Seven years later, a childhood friend reappeared at the moment I most needed him. I had been in America for only two months. An agency was supporting me, but soon I would have to support myself. I did not know how to support myself. I read newspapers and magazines all day long. I wanted to learn idioms. I wanted to become a real American. Chew the fat. Blow off some steam. Close but no cigar. Rings a bell. I must have sounded ridiculous. I only wanted to be natural. I gave up on that.

I had not seen him since I lost everything. I had not thought of him. He and my older sister, Anna, were friends. I came

upon them kissing one afternoon in the field behind the shed behind our house. It made me so excited. I felt as if I were kissing someone. I had never kissed anyone. I was more excited than if it had been me. Our house was small. Anna and I shared a bed. That night I told her what I had seen. She made me promise never to speak a word about it. I promised her.
She said, Why should I believe you?
I wanted to tell her, Because what I saw would no longer be mine if I talked about it. I said, Because I am your sister.
Thank you.
Can I watch you kiss?
Can you watch us kiss?
You could tell me where you are going to kiss, and I could hide and watch.
She laughed enough to migrate an entire flock of birds. That was how she said yes.
Sometimes it was in the field behind the shed behind our house. Sometimes it was behind the brick wall in the schoolyard. It was always behind something.
I wondered if she told him. I wondered if she could feel me watching them, if that made it more exciting for her.
Why did I ask to watch? Why did she agree?
I had gone to him when I was trying to learn more about the forced laborer. I had gone to everyone.
To Anna's sweet little sister,
Here is the letter you asked for. I am almost two meters in height. My eyes are brown. I have been told that my hands are big. I want to be a sculptor, and I want to marry your sister. Those are my only dreams. I could write more, but that is all that matters.
Your friend,
Thomas

I walked into a bakery seven years later and there he was. He had dogs at his feet and a bird in a cage beside him. The seven years were not seven years. They were not seven hundred years. Their length could not be measured in years, just as an ocean could not explain the distance we had traveled, just as the dead can never be counted. I wanted to run away from him, and I wanted to go right up next to him.
I went right up next to him.
Are you Thomas? I asked.
He shook his head no.
You are, I said. I know you are.
He shook his head no.
From Dresden.
He opened his right hand, which had NO tattooed on it.
I remember you. I used to watch you kiss my sister.
He took out a little book and wrote, I don't speak. I'm sorry.
That made me cry. He wiped away my tears. But he did not admit to being who he was. He never did.
We spent the afternoon together. The whole time I wanted to touch him. I felt so deeply for this person that I had not seen in so long. Seven years before, he had been a giant, and now he seemed small. I wanted to give him the money that the agency had given me. I did not need to tell him my story, but I needed to listen to his. I wanted to protect him, which I was sure I could do, even if I could not protect myself.
I asked, Did you become a sculptor, like you dreamed?
He showed me his right hand and there was silence.
We had everything to say to each other, but no ways to say it.
He wrote, Are you OK?
I told him, My eyes are crummy.

He wrote, But are you OK?

I told him, That's a very complicated question.

He wrote, That's a very simple answer.

I asked, Are you OK?

He wrote, Some mornings I wake up feeling grateful.

We talked for hours, but we just kept repeating those same things over and over.

Our cups emptied.

The day emptied.

I was more alone than if I had been alone. We were about to go in different directions. We did not know how to do anything else.

It's getting late, I said.

He showed me his left hand, which had YES tattooed on it.

I said, I should probably go home.

He flipped back through his book and pointed at, Are you OK?

I nodded yes.

I started to walk off. I was going to walk to the Hudson River and keep walking. I would carry the biggest stone I could bear and let my lungs fill with water.

But then I heard him clapping his hands behind me.

I turned around and he motioned for me to come to him.

I wanted to run away from him, and I wanted to go to him.

I went to him.

He asked if I would pose for him. He wrote his question in German, and it wasn't until then that I realized he had been writing in English all afternoon, and that I had been speaking English. Yes, I said in German. Yes. We made arrangements for the next day.

His apartment was like a zoo. There were animals everywhere. Dogs and cats. A dozen birdcages. Fish tanks. Glass boxes with snakes and lizards and insects. Mice in

cages, so the cats wouldn't get them. Like Noah's ark. But he kept one corner clean and bright.
He said he was saving the space.
For what?
For sculptures.
I wanted to know from what, or from whom, but I did not ask.
He led me by the hand. We talked for half an hour about what he wanted to make. I told him I would do whatever he needed.
We drank coffee.
He wrote that he had not made a sculpture in America.
Why not?
I haven't been able to.
Why not?
We never talked about the past.
He opened the flue, although I didn't know why.
Birds sang in the other room.
I took off my clothes.
I went onto the couch.
He stared at me. It was the first time I had ever been naked in front of a man. I wondered if he knew that.
He came over and moved my body like I was a doll. He put my hands behind my head. He bent my right leg a little. I assumed his hands were so rough from all of the sculptures he used to make. He lowered my chin. He turned my palms up. His attention filled the hole in the middle of me.
I went back the next day. And the next day. I stopped looking for a job. All that mattered was him looking at me. I was prepared to fall apart if it came to that.
Each time it was the same.
He would talk about what he wanted to make.
I would tell him I would do whatever he needed.

We would drink coffee.
We would never talk about the past.
He would open the flue.
The birds would sing in the other room.
I would undress.
He would position me.
He would sculpt me.
Sometimes I would think about those hundred letters laid across my bedroom floor. If I hadn't collected them, would our house have burned less brightly?
I looked at the sculpture after every session. He went to feed the animals. He let me be alone with it, although I never asked him for privacy. He understood.
After only a few sessions it became clear that he was sculpting Anna. He was trying to remake the girl he knew seven years before. He looked at me as he sculpted, but he saw her.
The positioning took longer and longer. He touched more of me. He moved me around more. He spent ten full minutes bending and unbending my knee. He closed and unclosed my hands.
I hope this doesn't embarrass you, he wrote in German in his little book.
No, I said in German. No.
He folded one of my arms. He straightened one of my arms. The next week he touched my hair for what might have been five or fifty minutes.
He wrote, I am looking for an acceptable compromise.
I wanted to know how he lived through that night.
He touched my breasts, easing them apart.
I think this will be good, he wrote.
I wanted to know what will be good. How will it be good?
He touched me all over. I can tell you these things because

I am not ashamed of them, because I learned from them. And I trust you to understand me. You are the only one I trust, Oskar.
The positioning was the sculpting. He was sculpting me. He was trying to make me so he could fall in love with me. He spread my legs. His palms pressed gently at the insides of my thighs. My thighs pressed back. His palms pressed out.
Birds were singing in the other room.
We were looking for an acceptable compromise.
The next week he held the backs of my legs, and the next week he was behind me. It was the first time I had ever made love. I wondered if he knew that. It felt like crying.
I wondered, Why does anyone ever make love?
I looked at the unfinished sculpture of my sister, and the unfinished girl looked back at me.
Why does anyone ever make love?
We walked together to the bakery where we first met.
Together and separately.
We sat at a table. On the same side, facing the windows.
I did not need to know if he could love me.
I needed to know if he could need me.
I flipped to the next blank page of his little book and wrote, Please marry me.
He looked at his hands.
YES and NO.
Why does anyone ever make love?
He took his pen and wrote on the next and last page, No children.
That was our first rule.
I understand, I told him in English.
We never used German again.
The next day, your grandfather and I were married.

POCKET PENGUINS

1. Lady Chatterley's Trial
2. **Eric Schlosser** Cogs in the Great Machine
3. **Nick Hornby** Otherwise Pandemonium
4. **Albert Camus** Summer in Algiers
5. **P. D. James** Innocent House
6. **Richard Dawkins** The View from Mount Improbable
7. **India Knight** On Shopping
8. **Marian Keyes** Nothing Bad Ever Happens in Tiffany's
9. **Jorge Luis Borges** The Mirror of Ink
10. **Roald Dahl** A Taste of the Unexpected
11. **Jonathan Safran Foer** The Unabridged Pocketbook of Lightning
12. **Homer** The Cave of the Cyclops
13. **Paul Theroux** Two Stars
14. **Elizabeth David** Of Pageants and Picnics
15. **Anaïs Nin** Artists and Models
16. **Antony Beevor** Christmas at Stalingrad
17. **Gustave Flaubert** The Desert and the Dancing Girls
18. **Anne Frank** The Secret Annexe
19. **James Kelman** Where I Was
20. **Hari Kunzru** Noise
21. **Simon Schama** The Bastille Falls
22. **William Trevor** The Dressmaker's Child
23. **George Orwell** In Defence of English Cooking
24. **Michael Moore** Idiot Nation
25. **Helen Dunmore** Rose, 1944
26. **J. K. Galbraith** The Economics of Innocent Fraud
27. **Gervase Phinn** The School Inspector Calls
28. **W. G. Sebald** Young Austerlitz
29. **Redmond O'Hanlon** Borneo and the Poet
30. **Ali Smith** Ali Smith's Supersonic 70s
31. **Sigmund Freud** Forgetting Things
32. **Simon Armitage** King Arthur in the East Riding
33. **Hunter S. Thompson** Happy Birthday, Jack Nicholson
34. **Vladimir Nabokov** Cloud, Castle, Lake
35. **Niall Ferguson** 1914: Why the World Went to War

POCKET PENGUINS

36. **Muriel Spark** The Snobs
37. **Steven Pinker** Hotheads
38. **Tony Harrison** Under the Clock
39. **John Updike** Three Trips
40. **Will Self** Design Faults in the Volvo 760 Turbo
41. **H. G. Wells** The Country of the Blind
42. **Noam Chomsky** Doctrines and Visions
43. **Jamie Oliver** Something for the Weekend
44. **Virginia Woolf** Street Haunting
45. **Zadie Smith** Martha and Hanwell
46. **John Mortimer** The Scales of Justice
47. **F. Scott Fitzgerald** The Diamond as Big as the Ritz
48. **Roger McGough** The State of Poetry
49. **Ian Kershaw** Death in the Bunker
50. **Gabriel García Márquez** Seventeen Poisoned Englishmen
51. **Steven Runciman** The Assault on Jerusalem
52. **Sue Townsend** The Queen in Hell Close
53. **Primo Levi** Iron Potassium Nickel
54. **Alistair Cooke** Letters from Four Seasons
55. **William Boyd** Protobiography
56. **Robert Graves** Caligula
57. **Melissa Bank** The Worst Thing a Suburban Girl Could Imagine
58. **Truman Capote** My Side of the Matter
59. **David Lodge** Scenes of Academic Life
60. **Anton Chekhov** The Kiss
61. **Claire Tomalin** Young Bysshe
62. **David Cannadine** The Aristocratic Adventurer
63. **P. G. Wodehouse** Jeeves and the Impending Doom
64. **Franz Kafka** The Great Wall of China
65. **Dave Eggers** Short Short Stories
66. **Evelyn Waugh** The Coronation of Haile Selassie
67. **Pat Barker** War Talk
68. **Jonathan Coe** 9th & 13th
69. **John Steinbeck** Murder
70. **Alain de Botton** On Seeing and Noticing